Our Lady of Lourdes C.H.S.

ANTHOLOGY
2017

A celebration of student creativity.
Edited by M. Reidel

i

CONTENTS

Living in the Moment

by MacKenzie Gibbings

For life is like a box of chocolates
As you never know what you're going to get
It may be good
It may be bad
But these are all just challenges
That you will pass for sure
For your heart and soul
Will forever be your own

You should think with your mind
But sometimes it may be wrong
For that is when you must
Believe and trust
In your heart and soul
For it will forever be your own

by Hayleigh King

Ocean Breeze

by Bryan Dyck

The fast blue ocean
That surrounds our world
The crashing wake
And tranquil waves
Washing away all imperfection
The salty taste and smell
Of the ocean breeze
The feeling of freedom
Amongst the endless leagues
Of blue wonder
Cold and hostile
Deep and fascinating
The biggest wonder of our world
New discoveries being made
Creatures new and old
Big and small
Our lifeblood
A mystery we have not deciphered

by Sarah Finoro

Decay

by Trent Peters

He erases entire stories.
No matter if they are old or young,
tall or short, popular and unpopular,
he does not care.
He'll erase your story leaving only a husk behind
to be put in the ground
and eaten b y worms.
This is a normal day for him.
He is emotionless.
He is… Death.

by Catherine Edwins

Free as a Bird

by Camille Manrique

What am I doing with myself? I'm lost
Aimlessly stagger down life's winding path
All I focus on is the risk and cost
On my journey accompanied by wrath
Wait, should I go left? Or should I go right
The choices I make will affect my life
All I know is I can't wait till daylight
But hey, I guess that is my endless strife
So much of my time is spent in the dark
I need to open my eyes for a start
I'll be able to breathe with my new spark
Because why live your life without a heart
Now I must continue my long journey
And act like a bird that has been set free

* * *

by Camille Smiderle

A breath of fresh air
perfect steps, smooth but present
Tracing through my mind

The Treeline

by Nick Skelton

BANG! Run. BANG! Run. BANG! Run.
"We'll find you!" Run.
The rough gravel path is too open.
I have to get to the treeline.
It appears as through it is a wall,
soft but rigid at the same time,
like you could easily slip into it,
but it would hurt on the way in.
Run. Once I'm inside,
all that is visible is the darkest imaginable green,
to the point that it almost mimics black
with indigo blue in the background.
BANG! Run. I slip on a root,
tangled in weeds trying to rip and thrash my way out.
I feel my skin peel and tear away at the razor –like thorns.
I break free. Run. I look behind to see that I am alone.
The wall of the treeline only let me through,
as if it was a barricade to the unwary
and a window to the heedful.
Walk. As I approach the willow tree to the east
I become more aware of the surroundings as my eyes adjust.
The woodland becomes more grim, yet welcoming in its own manner.
The almost path, like weed, align in a near flawless route to my destination.
Walk. I reach the tree. I sit and watch as the path I take becomes more clear.
It has been covered with a dark shadow, I look up and see no exit.
The treeline has been masked with a solid wall of trees,
engulfing the surrounding land.
I'm trapped. Stop.

Monday Morning

by Chloe Roberts

The sun coming through my window
Straight in my eye, like someone pointing a laser
The birds chirping bright and early
The smell of breakfast comes up slowly
Running through the whole house
My mind slowly waking up
The bags under my eyes tell it all
The taste of salt running down your face
Just getting up my legs feel like they're going to fall off
Walking like a turtle
Trying to get ready
Everything feels so slow
This is my Monday
Morning

* * *

by Vy Vu

While you just sit there,
I am working so hard by...
my blood sweat and tears.

Yellow Brick Road

by Roberta Carriere

Growing up I never chose my own favourite colour; I would just base it off of my friends'. If my best friends' favourite color was blue, mine would be blue, or if they changed their minds and changed it to pink, my new favourite would be pink. I would constantly change my favourite colour to fit in with other people's opinions. Not having a favourite colour made me feel like I was missing out on a secret club- where everyone had something special and I did not.

Saying I felt directionless without a favourite colour seems silly, but it was how I felt up until the age of 15. I never knew what colour to paint my room, or a colour to put when personality tests ask you,"What is your favourite colour?"

I felt this way until I finally found the colour, my colour. One day I was shopping after school and I walked into H&M in the hope of buying a couple of shirts. I walked through the store for about 5 minutes and I saw nothing that caught my eye. That was until I turned the corner and saw a dark yellow, long sleeve shirt. The shirt was practically calling my name.

I bought the shirt and nothing else. I hurried to pay and rushed home to put the shirt on. I felt like I finally had a connection with a colour that I never had before.

After I bought the shirt, I noticed that yellow was in everything; in flowers, in the sun, in paintings, in animals. It was everywhere and the more I saw yellow, the more the world became extremely beautiful.

Yellow, for me, is the sound of love songs and birds chirping. It is rays of sunshine on a hot summer day. It is the smell of bananas and the taste of lemon flavoured candy. It is the light in my dark days and it is everything to me.

Maybe I am crazy for having such a strong connection with a hue of the rainbow, but I hope everyone finds something that is their light in the darkness and their sound of love songs. I found my yellow brick road.

Hiding in the Headlights

by Camille Smiderle

"In four hundred metres turn left. In four hundred metres turn left. In four hundred me…" His eyes broke open to the sound of the familiar mechanical voice. His initial inhale singed his nostrils with the toxic stench of burnt rubber and hot blood. He felt dirt clinging to the sweat covering his trembling body and he could taste the humidity in the air. He felt it coating his lungs. Darkness encompassed him except for the faint yellowed glow of headlights creeping above the roads' edge. He was trapped. The only sounds that reached his ears were his own manic heartbeat and a few bystanding pebbles tumbling along the ground into nothingness. His sought after companion was sprawled lifelessly next to him, splintered with shards of glass. Her eyes were empty. His panicked thoughts of what was to come almost prevented him from hearing a gun cock beside his left ear, "Don't move."

"Clouded Thoughts" by Catherine Edwins

8

My World

by Andrew Nesbitt

Where I'd rather be is difficult to say
because it's not a place you can stay.
It's in the wind, you'll find
you're timed by the concentration inside.

The space is not whole, but perfectly patched places,
separate, but whole, is what inhabitants face.
Waiting, floating freely 'til my brain finds their place.

Some spaces last for years, while some are for weeks,
but every single space is never complete.
Some are on paper, cast to the earth,
while others lay dormant awaiting their birth.

Motifs carry over to give new life
when obsessions that carried them are decidedly rife
with points so plentiful
it would cause me to go mental.

Some days it seems the worlds aren't there at all.
It's like someone put up a wall.
But I can take solace in the fact
they will always come back.

In The Future

by Reanna Luccisano

In the future, **what's in store?**
No one knows, but we have an idea.
We ask ourselves questions.
What do we like?
What do we love?
What do we want to pursue?
Will I work in the town where I grew up,
or move and explore?
What inspires me?
Who will stand by me?
All these questions come and go,
until the day we need to know.
We need to make the decision and confirm.
We think thoughtfully and truthfully,
yet, still are not certain.
Eventually come to the conclusion.
What I chose is what I want.
That decision is in my hands.

by Cody Robinson

The Children

by Roberta Carriere

The children.

They laugh, they play, they scream.

The children.

They appear in the middle of your dreams.

The children

They seem to know all, way more than you think.

The children.

They see you wash away the pain with a drink.

The children.

They are everywhere, but nowhere at all.

The children.

They never see them, but you hear them call.

The children.

They are running.

The children.

They are coming.

* * *

by Ethan Lyons

Jesus on a cross
He was carved out of plastic
Looking down on me

Identity

by Emerson Hubble

I am who I want to be
Don't want to be any other way
Encouragement from a sea of familiar faces
No difference between them all
They call me, like sirens to sailors, for me to be like them
I am who I am
That is just who I want to be
You, need to find who you are

by Hayleigh King

My Magical Place

by Reanna Luccisano

Imagine a place that's special to you.
Somewhere you can relax, be free,
and let all your worries and frustrations disappear.
It's such a magical place.
For me it's the dance studio.
I walk into the studio
feel my toes touch the cool floor.
The room's empty and open.
I play music and start dancing,
feeling calm and at ease.
When I hear the melody
I feel the beat in my body.
Dancing by the wall of photos,
I smell hairspray and costumes,
like being at a recital.
I taste nervousness.
As I'm dancing, I express my feelings
when words can't.
After finishing, I sip water.
Going down my throat refreshingly.
I walk out of the studio with relief,
and get back to reality.

* * *

by Catherine Edwins

I long for your tight embrace,
and to see your sweet face.
My candied cardio-vascular pump system
or in other words, soul mate.

Love is a Flame

by Camille Smiderle

Love, is a flame.
It's intense, fierce and alluring.
It's curing to the soul one day at a time
until soon you find
you're left without a sign
of what happened to you two.

Seems he finally withdrew.

No.
Love isn't curing, it's stirring, it's worn.
It'll shake you to your core.
So let you be warned,
it'll swallow you up, like nothing has before.
Before you know it, you're left in it's dust,
with nothing and no one around to trust.

Alone,
With nothing still to discuss

Left,
in the charred black past, that was once on fire.

* * *

by Mackenzie Tucker

Inspiration is
a flame of fire growing fierce
and never burns out

Dandelion

by Tiffany Clarke

I lay still, hearing the wind scratch every blade of grass surrounding my delicate body. I feel my veins echo my heartbeat as the sun warms every drop of my blood. That rush of rouge rises solely from the consequence of this man. I am a daisy in a world of corruption and disease. He is my dandelion staying planted by my side just long enough to watch me blossom.

We cannot go very far, yet we are as free as every bird passing over us. Letting the wind take us whichever direction it pleases. I see him look to me out of the corner of my eye. His eyes are like a treasure chest at the bottom of the ocean. A beautiful gold surrounded by this enchanting sea green. I have never seen them so bright, he was beaming.

His large yet gentle demeanor stood up and closed the distance between us encasing me into his welcoming embrace. His rough fingertips graze across the soft silk of my dress as he wisps me up from the comfort of the ground, yet... I feel indestructible. In that moment, he taught me what it is like to fly.

His breathing quickens as he abruptly places me on the ground. Although he attempted to be gentle, his actions mirrored those of a jock who just won his first football game. He plummets to his knees leaving harsh green stains along his blue jeans. Hands ripping a few blades of grass up from their roots.

I see his veins trying to push their way out of his skin, desperate to find relief. I feel the sting in my eyes as my pupils dilate. I'm not focused on my red elbow quickly spreading to a tender purple. All I can think about is the darkness corrupting him as I watch his eyes go from an enchanting gold to a dull muddy brown. I slowly rise and take a small step towards him.

I feel the grass tickling my feet, but it is now cold, sending chills up my spine making every hair on the back of my neck stand on end. I hesitate before moving any closer, knowing if I act too quickly, I may irritate the beast corrupting my dandelion. His hunched posture softens, and without any further hesitation, I grasp his large arm with my petite ones. I am gently pulled away by a pair of arms I feel no need to identify in this moment.

I watch him enter the car before it speeds down the long dirt road, and my mother finally enters my vision. She tries to talk to me but she isn't making sense. I hear her repeat "everything is going to be fine", yet her eyes pour into mine with a red yet ghostly manner. She rests her hands on my shoulders trying to shield the shaking in her arms.

Minutes pass and our shivers begin to subside. I feel my tense shoulders loosen as I imagine him walking through that backdoor, ready to begin playing again. I may be a naive child, but I have an idea of what might be approaching me. My eyebrows furrow as I wonder what I should be feeling. Where did the infestation of butterflies that usually engulf me go? Why am I not frantically sweating? My eyes are still shimmering and gold. And this purple contaminating my elbow feels like an illusion.

I did love him, he cared for me. Cooked. Cleaned, and entertained me. I have never met a man like him. One minute he would be soaring through space plucking the stars just to provide me with, the next minute picking the dirt from under his rough nails. He did his best to keep those times from me, although he wasn't perfect at that. I usually saw him when he was gleaming. They tried to hide it from me, but I could feel the absence. My dandelion was turning from bright yellow to a dull grey awfully fast. Next thing I knew his aged petals drifted into the clouds as the wind carried him to live with the stars. Petal-by-petal. I guess my dandelion couldn't stay for the whole season. I'll never forget how he taught me how to fly. Now it's his turn. At least he will be truly free forever now.

16

Wildflower

by Ireland Heyden

We're in the kitchen. Her back is turned toward me; her hands
fixated on the mashed bananas she's fixing.
I can smell the banana bread cooking in the oven.
The rocking chair is set perfectly in front of the window; a
blurred silhouette from my memory.
If I stand on my toes, I'm just able to see over the pine trees in
the backyard.
Sunshine cuts through the glass; warming my face.
Yellow ribbons of light spreading across my cheeks – tugging at
the ends of my hair.
Yesterday the ribbons were grey.
Mother said that good things come out of thunderstorms; like
free car washes and watered plants.
Sooner or later the sun will come out

Mother is always right.
Her voice is Chamomile tea with honey
She's chocolate covered strawberries with vanilla ice-cream
She glows.
Her fingertips are touching the sun
Rays bouncing off her crooked teeth and untamed hair
She's a wildflower.
A finger painting in a world of cut and pasted photographs.
And daddy says I remind him of her

Daddy and I used to dance around in circles until we went dizzy
White tiles like the keys on a piano
I could have laid there for hours, just listening to the radio play
Jack Johnson's voice filling the empty spaces of my mind.
I'd always close my eyes; the memories so familiar
The warmth of the sunlight, the scent of banana bread, the music,
mother's soft voice
And daddy's lying beside me.
His steady breathing; like waves against the shoreline

I can almost hear his heartbeat
We're still.
Heads intertwined in a dance of simplicity

* * *

Daddy works a lot…
I rarely ever see him anymore.
His hair has gotten longer
Dirt filling the cracks of his hands like chocolate icing
Lips are redder than usual.
His collar hides circles of burgundy stamped along his neck
He reeks of cologne.
And I can hear Mum's voice again
She calls daddy
His body tenses.
Knuckles turn white.
Hot air closes in on me
I'm numb.

Not again.

Daddy's yelling now.
Sharp words stinging my ears
The cupboards slamming shut.
I close my eyes. Stay still.
This storm will pass.
It has before.

Mum is crying now.
Stay still.
I listen for the snap.

* * *

… nothing.
Silence.
Daddy's heavy breathing.

Clouds form in my eyes as rain starts trickling down my
cheeks.
The rag doll falls to the floor.

Snap.

* * *

Mother says that good things come out of thunderstorms; like
free carwashes and watered plants.
Sooner or later the sun will come out.
But something tells me..

* * *

I don't think she was talking about the weather.

Art Gallery

by Angelika Brzezinski

As I gripped the door's cold handle,
against my body I felt a whoosh of heat.
Walking in, quiet whispering is all I could hear.
Some admire the wonderful artwork in silence,
others share their opinions aloud.
I approach a 3D copper apple,
the texture felt so cool.
It seemed I could almost taste the sour juice.
Next to me was a tall, fancy dressed man,
I could smell his spicey cologne hitting me.
Just sitting…
and admiring all the art I see
in silence, is all I need.
Yet, hearing the passion in someone's voice
as they analyze art is inspiring.

Florida Dreamin'

by Melissa Vongphakdy

Sunny, palm trees, warm sand, and weather
The glow of the sun on your skin
And the heat of the sand between your toes
Relaxing by the ocean, hearing waves crash
The moist air blowing through your hair
Getting into the tepid ocean
You can taste the saltiness
Feel the wave hovering over your body as you swim
Emerge to feel the sand stick to the bottom of your feet
Walk to get your favourite ice cream
Taste the cold against the warmth of your tongue
Watch it drip down the cone's side and drop to the ground
Stroll on the boardwalk, smell the ocean breeze
Along the shore, leave your footprints
Waves come in and wash them away
Feel the water on your feet, look out into the crystal clear sea
As the bright, hot sun shines on your face
Seagulls fly high in the sky
Standing in the sand, listening to the waves
Watching the birds fly and palm trees bend
Feeling so relaxed, thinking about the sunset
Watching people swim in the ocean
Lay on the sand, feel the rays of the sun heating your body
You're golden brown, your hair wavy and your body is warm
Now, it's time to watch the sun fade away
Your Florida dreamin' has come to an end

by Mackenzie Tucker

Puzzling me why it is so powerful

Overcoming anger, sadness and fear

Squeezing sadness slowly out of the picture

Implanting smiles on people's faces

Trapping my madness in a dark locked room

Impacting my day one minute at a time

Victory dances on my bed at the end of the day

Increasing the happiness of others

Targeting my next day like a game of Battleship

Yet to wonder if it will be as good as today

* * *

by Melany Michaud

Happiness feels good
But happiness can be lost
When you leave the light

"At Work" by Ryan Pham

Butterfly Jewels
by Kira Nesbitt

Bad luck beautifully
Amber-encased
Metalmark butterflies trapped clinging
Hardened

Found Poem Source: National Geographic magazine

The Night Sky

by Athena Langhorn

The night sky is deep like the ocean,
endless like the universe
and complicated like the particles that make it up,
the night sky is quiet as the clouds
and the gentle shades of blue that enclose it,
It stands still, but moves like light,

The sky sings the song of mystery,
hums the tune of loneliness and
shines the suns of forgiveness,

The night sky is there always,
Reflecting, consuming the earth's
waters and winds, collecting the
people's dreams;
The people who stare up at the somber
sky from below. The night sky is a mystery, a secret that
Is known only by the angels who make its stars shine.

The Shootout

by Joshua Romero

Can you see it?
The net and metal frame
Mesh swaying in the wind
Like a child on a swing

Can you smell it?
The fear, anxiety, anxiousness
Sweat and emotions
Freshly cut grass just for your liking

Can you taste it?
The victory you've worked so hard for
What it feels like to be as champion, or… defeat
All your team's hard work on your shoulders
Their fate lies with you

Can you feel it?
You must make this shot!
The crowd is cheering, chanting your name
Feet stomping, hands clapping
Makes the ground tremor

Can you feel it?
The sun beams, its warmth pecking your skin
You take a deep breath and then
A sudden rush of adrenaline flows
Throughout your body

Can you feel it?
Your heart starts pumping, pumping, pumping
It feels like it's gonna burst from your chest
Your start to run, towards the ball…

Armour Piercing Questions

by Kira Nesbitt

I was only 15 when my heart turned to ice.
Like Prometheus and the eagles,
every night repose would thaw my heart.
But come the sun's travel across the day,
awareness would freeze my heart once more.
Years have come and gone,
and every time a great evil arose.
My heart froze more and more,
'til it turned to solid ice.
The world became wicked.
Good outweighed by the sinful tenfold.
Hope died one year ago.
Even you, O Lord, have become spiteful.
The cruel live too long,
The kind die too soon.
You have become uncaring,
when we cry out to you,
"Save my Mother/Father/Sister/Brother/Child."
You roll your eyes.
I denounce you!
How can I trust you
when you stole my mother from her kin and children?
You are a coward!

But the curse you put on me is breaking.
My heart is slowly thawing.
You wanted me to be in pain,
but I will rise once more
like a phoenix from the ashes.
You will know the wrath of a Nesbitt.
Your puppetry of life will backfire.
You will regret it.
I will laugh.
You made the wicked!
You made war!
You made hate!
So why should I feel sorry for you
when you didn't consider my feelings before?

Summer Love

by Roberta Carriere

The golden sun touches my skin and my heart
The butterflies in my stomach want to be free
The water cools my warm cheeks
The feeling of love is irreplaceable

The butterflies in my stomach want to be free
Our fingers intertwined, never breaking loose
The feeling of love is irreplaceable
The sleepless nights were spent together

Our fingers intertwined, never breaking loose
The water cools my warm cheeks
The feeling of love is irreplaceable
The golden sun touches my skin and my heart

by Mimi Hannant-Steffler

In The Meadow

by Liethan Velaso

Sitting in front of my cabin in the meadow
The arms of the chair felt smooth in my hands
The front door hinge squeaked as it fluttered in the wind
Small windows reflected the image of the grassy field
A fire was crackling inside the fireplace
It's fiery tongues licked at the cauldron above
Within the cabin smelled of a juicy beef stew
Every spoonful filled my mouth with extravagant flavours

A bed lay in the corner
Silky sheets spread across a sturdy frame
A cloud of pillows rested on top
A table of memories, fun times, sad times
Stood in the middle of the wooden room
A candle flickered on top

Cabinets and closets of vinyl wood lined the walls
Storing utilitarian belongings
Lamps of glass and brass lit up the walls
Within them were their own life sources

Outside, grassy fields of radiant green
Reflected the white light of the sun, which penetrated by eyes
Flowers of the rainbow highlighted the fields with colour
The sweet fragrant nectar brought calm to my nose
Its petals were soft and carried the dew of the morning
Tall, firm trees stood like soldiers throughout the field
Its oak bark felt rough to the touch, filled with knots
Hefty leaves brought shade to the ground
I could hear birds chirping from the branches
Gracefully singing their hearts out into the morning

The breeze carried the scent of the sea, salt and water in one
I looked at everything and thought to myself
This… is a lovely place to relax
After placing the bowl of delicious stew on the counter
I slumped into the wooden rocking chair
And I closed my eyes
And drifted to sleep, and into the dream world
When I came to
I was greeted by loud noises outside
Noticing dark walls looming over myself
With fearsome apparitions
To my right, was a drawer, with a picture
In the picture was a cabin
I noticed a piece of bread
On the tiny table in front of me
I walked over… took a bite
It tasted stale and bland
Difficult to chew
I took a seat in a small chair
And sat there in silence
In my cold apartment

"Jada" by Jessica Matthieu

Trash Can

by Liethan Velaso

A trash can
Dirt and filth within the can's wall
Seagulls pecking at the waste
What's in the trash can? Emotions
Discarded, a ripped picture of a happy couple
Guilt, anger, sadness
The mitten of an abused child
Fear, loneliness, pain
A happy meal, half eaten
Crushed at the bottom of the trash can
It's smile distorted into a grimace
Happiness, fun, joy, discarded recklessly
Everyday people walk quickly by and toss them away
Feelings, possibilities, opportunities, potential
Trashed without a single thought
Within this trash can reside
The feelings of the broken and lonely
Within this trash can is one man's rubbish
Which should have been their treasure

* * *

by Andrew Nesbitt

Some things don't make sense
Like when the world disappeared
And left us to fight

Don't Play With Fire

by Anushka Massey

Infatuation is like a captivating flame, hard to tame
Radiates, yet frames
Comforting though blazes
Attractive but deceiving
It leads you to things you'd never think of doing
Fire is like an addictive drug
It can be the most beautiful when ready
But… if it is not ready, you'll get burned
Feeding the fire makes it stronger
It can spread like wildfire, if not handled carefully
When left unchecked, with no boundaries,
Fire cannot last forever,
One minute it's there and the next it's blown out

* * *

by Emerson Hubble

She lights up my life
She is a rose among thorns
I am hers to keep

Auschwitz

by Rachael Gemin

Separated from family and torn from your life.
Isolated from the world; felt cut like a knife.

Living day-by-day with uncertainty and fear,
while witnessing the deaths of your peers.

A number they gave you, representing whom you are.
You mourn your family who are gone afar.

Praying each morning that you will not be picked,
hope for something gentle, like being brutally kicked.

The labour that you did for the sergeant's and the camp,
they didn't appreciate, then your clothes were all damp.

They treated you like a rag doll since your life didn't matter,
And laughed amongst themselves with their ugly, racist chatter.

You felt for that little girl, screaming for her mom.
You didn't have the heart, to tell her she was gone.

The little food you ate didn't put meat on your bones,
Everyday you felt dead, lost and alone.

All of the corpses you saw… devastating but true.
You prayed to God that it would not be you.

There were so many events that those people witnessed,
To survive such conditions, they were truly blessed.

We remember the prisoner of Auschwitz in our hearts.
And hope that in heaven they'll never be apart.

Autumn Leaves

by Camille Smiderle

Her electrifying eyes lured me towards her with a single beckoning finger
A sense of wonder wrapped itself around the heartbeat of my mind
The width of my hand fit the curve of her face like a perfect puzzle piece
Her soothing voice smoothed over the rough concrete of my inhibitions

A sense of wonder wrapped itself around the heartbeat of my mind
I could feel my thoughts being delicately swirled in loose circles like autumn leaves
Her soothing voice smoothed over the rough concrete of my inhibitions
Endless conversations filled the warm air with sweet nothings and new hope

I could feel my thoughts being delicately swirled in loose circles like autumn leaves
The width of my hand fit the curve of her face like a perfect puzzle piece
Her soothing voice smoothed over the rough concrete of my inhibitions
Her electrifying eyes lured me towards her with a single beckoning finger

* * *

by Kira Nesbitt

Hope can be like a
nightingale in the dark night
unknown and unsure

In my Hand

by Jassmeen Banger

In my hand lays a diploma, crisp and brand new,
a paper that reminds me what I already knew.
The time of childish games has come to an end,
those I've known for so long, will no longer be friends.
The start of adulthood is not far from reach,
yet here I sit with this melancholy screech
nerves are still unsettled from the night before
keeping me awake until half past four.
Where I will go after this is still undetermined
but I will be ready when it is confirmed.
Until then, let me rest in this moment of mine
as I hold my future for the first time.

* * *

by Sarah Finoro

Soft, warm place to stay
I know it sounds so cliché.

But in the dark of the night,
you are there to hold me tight.

Diary Of A Refugee

by Athena Langhorn

Diary Entry Number One

If there is one thing anyone should know about me, it is that I always have a plan and I always know what to do. I remember every single detail about that night. It repeats in my mind, it lingers in my soul and runs through my blood, it is a part of me now, it's my new life. I can still hear the echoes of the crash that woke me. I remember my mother's trembling hand reaching for me. I hear the cries of my neighbours, my loved ones, my family. I remember my heart racing, my body shaking. I remember the pain, confusion, hot gravel burning my bare feet as we fled the flaming village and splashed into the river. My mother's words came out quivering and cautious, but her tone told me they were imperative. "Take your sister. Go now, before it's too late! Mr. Kahlid is at the river. He'll take you to safety. Your father and I must stay and help. We will take another raft after we make sure all the children are safe." I remember resisting, insisting to wait for them, the pain in my mother's eyes. She was the strongest person I knew, a leader, and to see her scared tore me apart. I remember struggling to comfort my sister when I could barely comprehend the event myself. But mostly, I remember the regret that numbed me for weeks. I remember the small life raft drifting away from the rugged fishing port. I remember the bomb, the ground shaking and the vibrant orange of the blazing village. The searing heat of the flames on my face, and then, nothing.

At that moment I was too shaken to feel anything. I just held on to my terrified 6 year-old sister, who'd witnessed her village perish in a rage of hot flames. I shut my eyes tight and cried, something I seldom allowed myself to do, as I believed it displayed weakness. It wasn't until now that I realized crying was a way of becoming stronger and not holding on to my sadness, because *that* would have made me weak. The wind was bitter and raw. It blew the raft about forcefully and encouraged the icy water to jump into the boat. I was panicking. I couldn't believe what just happened was real life. I kept expecting to wake up and realize it was all just a dream, a nightmare. I was short of breath and had a massive headache. I hurt. I hurt for my parents, I hurt for my sister, I hurt for my village and but most of all I hurt for myself. I felt awful that I was safe and thousands of others were not. All of me was numb, frozen, and yet I was safe. I should have been happy. I tried to steady my breathing, to stop shaking, but I couldn't. It happened so fast. A million thoughts ate away at my mind as I tried to get comfy and warm in our small corner of the raft, but gushes already started collecting and before I knew it I was sitting in cold water. My legs ached, my stomach was empty and my clothes were wet. For the first time in my life, my head was completely blank and I didn't know what to do.

Diary Entry Number Two

When I woke up it was light. The air was warm, and the sky was a soft blue with streaks of pinky-orange. Everything was too sweet and bright for the kind of pain that ached inside me. We were about to arrive somewhere and we'd be expected to continue our lives like nothing happened. I was scared. I had no idea where we were going and how I was supposed to be the strong one. My mother had always been a leader, courageous and compassionate. It was as if nothing scared her, she was always kind and willing to help. And now she was gone... We were on our own and I had to look after Aria. I had to make sure nothing else happened to her. All of the sudden a rush of anger filled me. I was mad at my parents for staying behind, mad at the adults, the "leaders" that caused the conflict and cost me everything I cared about. The only thing I had left was Aria. I couldn't let her down, but how could I support her? I glanced at her, curled up in a little ball breathing gently. I made a promise to myself, right there in that life raft on our way to a new beginning, one with an unfortunate purpose. I promised myself that if I couldn't be strong for me, I would be for Aria. This was a chance for us to live out our lives, to become something. And it was up to me to care for my sister, to be resilient and be the leader that mom always was. Then I felt strong; I felt strength from God and from my parents. I knew they needed me to have faith and open my mind and heart to whatever and whoever awaited us in this new place. I knew, no matter how hard this experience was going to be, that it was the right thing and my parents wouldn't have wanted me to be scared. Then, Aria opened her eyes slowly as she breathed in the cool morning air. I could see the fear in her eyes. I took a deep breath. "No more sadness," I whispered, and for a moment, an assured smile glimmered on her tiny face.

When the raft finally reached land, we were free. Not physically, but mentally. I was free, my spirit was free and I was free of anger and sadness. I had felt such a strong connection earlier, as if my mother was in my soul whispering "be strong" any time I felt weak and unsure of what to do. I swear, as we trudged up the grassy bank, I could hear my mother speaking to me. "You are capable of everything that will come your way, don't doubt yourself my darling Mayhai. You are stronger than you ever have been before, after all, you always know what to do…" I took Aria's hand and we walked together to a new life.

The land here is very much the same as it was back in Syria. Grassy, rolling hills and twisting, sandy paths. The sky is the same bright blue except the dull layer of smoke from the bombs is no longer lingering. The people who greeted us at the shore lead us to a large, dry field of brown sand and yellow grass. They separated the adults from the children and brought our group, of about 12 children, into one of the tents. There we gave them our names, received immigrant cards and a few vaccinations. We were given 2 food vouchers and a wagon full of supplies like rope, knives, plates, glasses, clothing and toiletries. When we were done in the tents, they grouped us up and assigned us living quarters. The children who had made it here with their parents were reunited with them and sent in the opposite direction as us. My heart ached, a single tear sunk out of my eye and trickled down my face. But I stopped because all could picture was my mother, disappointed in my weakness. We were the misfits, but we had made it this far, and I wasn't going to give up hope now. There were 8 children and 5 adults left over. We were split among 2 tents. In our tent there were two ladies Ms. Nashua and Mrs. Larur, one younger probably in her twenties, and the other older, probably mid-thirties. The older one had her son, a young boy called Cabot, with her. The younger woman was to look after two young orphaned children. One girl, Miriyama, and one boy, Bourck; they were not related. And I was to protect Aria and myself, being fifteen I was old enough to look after Aria, otherwise we might have been separated.

Diary Entry Number Three

I try my best to have a good attitude about the living conditions and all the new people, but I am nervous because everything is different here. After all, we don't know anyone in this camp except Mr. Kahalid who is on the other side of the premises. We don't know whom we can trust. Everything in this camp is durable and screams survival. Back at home, in our cozy, rural village, our house was sturdy, but welcoming. There were always a bunch of colourful flowers dappling our front walkway and soft rolling hills hugged our lot. At the camp everything is bare and flat. The dirt here is always wet from the rain it absorbs. I figure we were somewhere in Europe, but not too far away from Syria, because the boat ride was pretty short. I asked Mr. Kahalid, our family friend that had travelled in the raft behind us. He told me that we were at Camp Urfa, in Turkey. I had never heard of a country called Turkey, nor had I known that it was so close to Syria. The camp is set up with the main office/headquarters in the far corner, with the two tents we entered directly after arriving. There are larger tents around the perimeter, which we guessed are for the people that own the camp, and in the center of the camp are the tents that we live in. The tents are positioned very close to one and other in an array, with clothing lines and packages clustered about each one. In our section, tents housing 5-10 people are long and have high, pointed roofs. The material is a rough, grey fabric that is water resistant. There are hundreds of tents in our section and there are even more across the field. If I stand at the very edge of our camp, I can see a tiny row of gray tips in the distance.

After we were assigned a tent and had officially met our neighbours, we began to unpack some of the materials we were given earlier. In our tent we set up a small dining area and a place to assemble and cook food on our tiny camp stove. There are 4 small, dirty mattresses, set up as bunk beds, in the back of our tent our supplies and clothing stay lined up in a neat order along one wall. Health clinics are provided in the larger tents close to the headquarters so that if someone falls ill they have access to medicine. We can go to a showering station and Laundromat twice each week and Aria and Bourck get to go to school. I had the option of education, but I'm already very educated as I have had 8 years of schooling back at home. I can read and write and I know some easy math, but I have always wanted to be a housewife, now I can be! Ms. Nashua and Mrs. Larur work for 7 hours each day at the other camp, which is apparently bigger and even has a little street full of shops. While they are at work earning money, I look after one of the orphaned children, Miriyama, and Mrs. Larur's baby, Cabot. While I am at home, I do other chores and household maintenance jobs like washing dishes and clothes, cooking and collecting water from the well that is shared among our section of about 30 tents. When Ms. Nashua and Mrs. Larur got their jobs at the shops in the larger camp north of here, a man told me that I could work in the future too. There are fields for crops that need tending to and gardens and shops. So when the children are a bit older I can have my own job. If we are still here... If the conflict ends, Aria and I will have no one to go home to. What will we do? I don't know. I am still extremely dismal, but each day I wake up and am able to eat and wear decent clothing. I am not cold and I am healthy. That is all that matters for now.

Diary Entry Number Four

This morning I woke with a start. For the first time since the night we left, Miriyama was banging her spoon on a series of dented, copper pans. I dragged myself out of bed, put a new dress on and made us a lovely breakfast of bread, and my favourite thing about this camp, strawberry jam. The people at one of the market shops make it when the strawberries in the garden come into season. I would like to work in the garden one day, creating and controlling life and turning it into something delicious. I snap out of my daydream and put Miriyama on the mat to play with some toys that were donated for a while. I feed baby Cabot, clean him up, change him and put him down for a short nap. Then I take Miriyama and our wagon with three pails to the little well around the bend. I gather water and leave Miriyama to play a little while longer while I wash the clothes at the Laundromat. When I come back I make lunch of rice, bread and beans. Then I begin to prepare water and other ingredients for supper. Piayaya, which is salmon, sausages and vegetables in rice, was something we used to eat back at home, with bread. This meal is no longer purely memories, it's survival.

Diary Entry Number Five

I love that I am of use here and can help our new family, but the days are seldom exciting. I have too much free time and nothing to do with it. Back at home I would attend school. I wrote stories with a computer program and they would bring my tales to life. I watched T.V. and I painted my nails. Here, I am lost in my thoughts and in my time. Today, when I was making dinner, Miriyama woke up from her nap and wandered into the kitchen area. She wanted me to play, but I couldn't so I told her a story. As I described the characters and places and problems in my tale, I painted a picture of the scenes in our minds. I loved that I was able to share my writing. Through this I realized that even though things are different now, I still have substance, purpose and people who love and depend on me. Whether or not I like everything about this life, I am part of something here at Urfa. If one thing is certain, it is my uncertainty of the future that will keep me engaged in life, through the good times and the bad.

"Weathered" by Adam Barr

Monsters

by Cierra Mandeville-Jordan

A monster will not look like a monster. It will not be obvious they are evil. They will look like you, talk like you. They will not start off acting like a monster. No, they wouldn't get anything they want if they did it that way.

Instead, they'll do the opposite. They will make you feel safe, secure, happy even. They'll tell lies that you would never expect to be lies, because it's already too late. They've earned your trust, and now they want you to think that they trust you too. They'll tell you their darkest secrets. Enough secrets to make you believe that they need your support, that they need your love, and you'll give it to them.

You'll believe that you're in control, when in reality you're so tightly wrapped around their finger that you've lost the ability to breathe. Your vision is failing and now you're gone blind.

You can't see that what they're doing to you is wrong. You're so stuck in that idea that you love them, that you don't want anyone else. Or, does no one else want you?

By the time you realize what's happened, you'll believe you're so far broken that no one could ever fix you. The only one who understands you is the one who moulded you into this. So, you keep going back. You seek more comfort in being understood than you do in the idea of starting all over.

You seek cover in this monster that has not only taken your identity from you, but has given you a new one. That's just the way they want it. You never saw it coming, because they don't look like a monster. They look like you. They talk like you.

True Connections

by Anushka Massey

The most beautiful people show kindness
Eventually, people can become crushed
The pitch, black night can cause others blindness
True love is best when people are not rushed
In darkest places there is always light
Relationships build on patience and trust
Work at something you love with all your might
Having a clear perspective is a must
Relationships are not flowers and rainbows
Like trees they can wilt or could grow fruitful
Each and every kinship will juxtapose
Trust is built on people being truthful
It's always nice to see others grinning
Don't worry it's only the beginning

"Keep it Locked" by Ryan Pham

Insightful Obscurities

by Camille Manrique

You spent your days trapped in the dark
Living your life stuck in the past
Wondering when you'll finally make you mark
But you always forget that life does not last

You've sat in silence, through thick and thin
Yet darling, you've committed but one crime
Not lies, theft, nor sin
But that you've run out of time

As the days retreat
Your time has come
Just know you're beat
And you feel nothing, but numb

It's time for it to be said
You've done well, you hid
But, can you really be dead
When you've never lived?

Burnt Out Flame

by Camille Manrique

Kaia Parker... Undoubtedly the most popular and richest girl at school. She strutted down the hallways with a sense of pride, as if she was walking the runway for Tyra Banks. She was easy to identify even in the largest crowd. Her long blonde hair shone like the golden fields of New Zealand, while her amber eyes glowed like sunshine going through a glass of whiskey. She was pure perfection. With a voice like a siren's call, men were helplessly drawn to her. She was known to be a promiscuous woman, with a new boyfriend on her arm every week. It seemed understandable. Once you gaze into those enchanting amber eyes, however, you see past the warm facade she has created, because eyes truly are the window to the soul. Kaia was lonely. Her parents were never home; loving their jobs more than their children. Although Kaia was rich and could buy anything she batted an eye at, none of it made her happy. Why be wealthy when you have no one to share it with. Her "boyfriends" were used to fill the emotional void that wasn't apparent growing up. Her appearance was always well groomed in hope of earning her peer's recognition and envy. She had many things going for her; smart, kind, beautiful. She was a triple threat, but never measured up to her parents expectations. Kaia dedicated her life to create an image of her happiness, but that light has long burnt out.

* * *

by Emerson Hubble

Language, the great wall
Language keeps people apart
But unites like minds

U-NI-VER-SI-TY

by Nam Nguyen and Kenton Tran

Waiting anxiously
I can't eat, I can't sleep
Not knowing when it'll be
The time I receive the news
The days turn into weeks
The weeks turned into months
Someone, someone, Help! Help me please!
This is a slam poem
Of how our lives are decided
By a mere letter of compliance
Numbers, numbers and more numbers
Our life is decided by a mere number on a piece of paper
Isn't out life worth more than this?
We aren't defined by numbers
We have emotions and memories and opinions
We love we hate we feel
To talk back against a society
That only wants numbers
What can a mere person do?
Against the social norm of the billions

The Call of Freedom

by James Dixon

Bones crack under weight of liberation
Battles many times fought, many times won
With each blank slate we promote creation
Yet new hatred would see our work undone

Authority sustained by tyranny
Us vulnerable are cruelly oppressed
Those who silence us cry conspiracy
And deny factors that lead to unrest

We rise to the sound of revolution
They incite fear, we start organizing
To their problem we find the solution
Uproot rusted systems through uprising

If you listen you hear the coming storm
A new generation's social reform

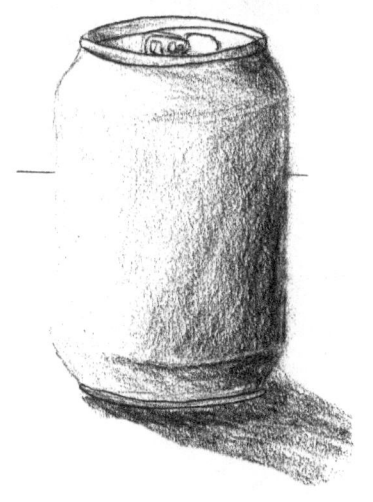

by Lucas Bernhard

45

The Bluebird's Song

by Camille Smiderle

A rose.
Beautiful,
but it can't survive on it's own.
Seeds sown
still need water and sun,
but sometimes the rays that are supposed to lift you up
are the ones that burn you to the ground.
I needed you to breathe.
I needed your hand in mine to feel at ease.
I needed your light, my intentions to appease
yet I could feel the dandelioned breeze
of life and my own individuality passing me by.
With every second you had your gloved hand wrapped around my heart.
Yet I stayed.
Your static, delicate flower, four whole seasons,
for reasons I could not tell you today.
But hey,
everyone makes mistakes these days.
Mistakes can haunt, you know.
They can show every crack
in your concrete
that you've been trying to stuff with useless excuses.
They can throw you against the wall of truth with one hand
and strip you of protective thorns with the other.
Standing before you,
smothering you in it's cold shade.
I wanted to be that girl.
Trust me I did,
I hid

all the things I knew you didn't like
I became just lifelike enough
for them to think I was happy,
never too sappy
and always well behaved.
Caved in,
with your name engraved in
every action,
never fading once,
just like those sun rays.
But soon I knew every ray you shone made me weaker,
I was immune to the speaker
of reason and everything the voice inside my head
used to tell me I deserved.
I was reserved, wilted and worn.
But I was never your flower.
I was the sun
taking form in something you thought
you could keep close and control
but the toll
you took on me was only a fraction of the whole
of who I am.
I should've never cowered so small.
I was the master of my downfall.
unaware of how powerful my light was,
how strong I was,
of how beautiful the bluebirds' song was,
unaware of how wrong you were.
You can scour the earth for me,
but the sun isn't something you could ever capture.

Forget

by Andrew Nesbitt

Forget
The stall was on the boardwalk like a bright red beacon
In the sea of sandy beige and deep blue
Forget
The song that played from it was almost addictive
But though the song was loud, the seagull were louder
The sound floating around in clumps
Rather than any distinguishable source
Forget
The smell is what you remember the most
It was so far from any other stall
It was all you could smell
The sweet aroma mixed with boiling oil
Forget
It was a humid heavy breath that filled your lungs
It felt like it got stuck there
Until you couldn't see the stall anymore
Forget
You can't remember
What it sold
Or why it was there
But you felt broken hearted when you left
Forgotten

Daughter to Mother

by Kira Nesbitt

I believe I am trapped in a hell
One that functions like a carousel
Round, round no way of being free
No matter how I cry, beg or plea
My screams fall to the deaf carny in charge
The burdens I wear as a crown grow large
Three years have chimed since then
When God forced you to Heaven
Anger and hate was born from your passing
But, I don't blame you for what is happening
One day I will be free from this maelstrom
And see you, who is too good for the sinful earth, Mom

by Tess Haverluck

Broken Bodies and Other Musings

by Ben Yoganathan

Broken bodies walk towards a dawn they are sure will one day wrap them i its arms. Broken people hang from the dreams of a world they thought wou know them better.

Shattered realities let blood slip from the wounds of their longing. Promise: are easy enough to remove from skin but cut like your mother's hand on a h afternoon.

Dreams let themselves out when you look elsewhere, but bruise like the ey of the kid you once walked through the night sky with.

Those same galaxies once shimmering in every word you pressed off your tongue to a girl that burned your mouth with desire.

Her mark is still here. Scars are strokes on a canvas you don't remember asking for. Bent edges closing in on themselves.

Severing the words you said to someone you weren't sure was listening. Lil a child pushing concrete behind their bike wheels because they feel the brakes between their fingers.

Knowing that you can stop makes flying seem like a dirty thing. Like stardust you don't remember finding under your jagged edges.

Like songs you forgot once held the universe together.

Like the misshapen parts of ourselves that we wrecklessly try to hold in ou imperfect stares. The same gazes of the people that once made our hearts burn as they rubbed broken memories with ours. Bodies colliding into bodies.

Folding into themselves. Touching what we can't say. Stories buried under the tree we used to climb to the very top of. All under a blanket of stars waiting like the warmth inside your mother's arms.

I like to think that we all turn into stars when we die. That the sky is just a giant mirror bent across everything, showing us how beautiful we all are, if we'd just look up. We bury the shards of ourselves so no one has to bleed trying to put us back together. But we all have pieces missing from a place we'd rather not remember. The universe is every piece of ourselves we bury. It is wherever we call home, it is every breath we place onto a lover's neck, every lost gaze from who we once were. It runs in our veins and bursts from our tears and gets stuck under our fingernails. We are children of space and although we are broken, stars glint off our dreams. We were never meant to be fixed or put back. We caress our tattered hope into a sky that shimmers. Songs fold over into themselves. When we burn we burn together. When we fall, we fall together. We are all singularities. The broken bodies of a place which demanded to exist. Our bones are in the sky. The stars in her eyes. We will all be a part of each other someday. The light will burn out but before it does we pull ourselves to the places where the words we sung still shatter a blinding light. Bruised into a new dawn. That holds us where nothing reaches. This place is in us as much as we are in it. And our shine can never be tamed.

by Mimi Hannant-Steffler

Before the Snow Sticks

by Camille Manrique

Times were different before the first layer of snow stuck to the ground
You enjoyed the hot summer air, and the sun that constantly kissed your skin
But I was like a snowflake, from the first squall
You didn't notice me until you had a closer look
See, I was different, I was unique
You would never be able to find another like me
I danced around, whenever the sun would shine I would gleam
Our time together was beautiful
but just like your love, winter came to an end
I let myself fall for you, and melt right into the palms of your hands
You let me slip through the gaps between your fingers
Because you knew
If you wanted another snowflake
You could just wait until next winter

by Monica Orlando

Open Your Mind

by Trent Peters

Your mind, the biggest place in the universe,
but you aren't born that way.
You have to open your mind for it to become that size.
So open your mind.
Minds are as silent as the wind rushing through a forest,
as empty as the driest desert,
as bright as a full moon on the clearest night of the year.
Open your mind.
You're anywhere you want,
even your most crazy dream.
Open your mind.
Go to the farthest fast food joint,
or rest on the closest couch.
Open your mind.
Travel through time and space
while laying on your bed
watching an intergalactic war live.
Hear gigantic explosions
like deafening noises of gears grinding.
Hear the soldiers scream for help
like the cries of starving children,
or shouts of victory.
Open your mind.
Taste the most delicious delicacies.
Such as crunchy crackers, crispy crustasceans, creamy crème brulee.
Taste a bowl of ice cream, with gilded flakes.
Eat it with a golden spoon,
like it's from the cleanest glacier with the purest vanilla.
Or pour yourself a drink so cold it burns your throat as if drinking fire.
Open your mind.
The possibilities are limitless.

Severed Connections

by Autumn Barnes

He was a street dweller, a nomad. A damp grey sweatshirt with gaping holes sheltered his regretful, dirt smeared face. The smell of cigarettes and mold saturated his tattered sweatshirt and torn jeans. His deep set eyes were fogged with sadness. Wrinkles as prominent as a crack in the street were etched into his weathered face. Skin clinged to his boney fragile frame, he sat hunched over on a collapsed cardboard box, using torn newspaper as warmth and shelter. His faint voice croaked, "Homeless... please help." All that was heard in response was the shuffling footsteps of disapproving passersby. Hopeless, homeless, he prayed for any sort help. Looked to strangers on the street for rescue. A rough childhood severed all familial connections. During his teenage years, his addiction became his only companion. Leading him to reside on the side of the street.

* * *

by Ethan Lyons

Should I stay, or leave?
I am nothing when I'm here
But it is strange there

Unexpected Assurance

by Camille Manrique

Their eyes stared into my soul
My hands were trembling and shaking
I was just waiting for this moment to end
As I was drowning in a wave of anxiety that had just engulfed me

My hands were trembling and shaking
But then I saw your sparkling green eyes, and I knew everything would be okay
As I was drowning in a wave of anxiety that had just engulfed me
I took a deep breathe and began my performance

But then I saw you, and I knew everything would be okay
I was just hoping for this moment to end
As I was drowning in a wave of anxiety that had just engulfed me
Their eyes stared into my soul

"QWERTY" by Malea Cruz-Diaz

Grief

by Catherine Edwins

The Five Stages of Grief; Denial, Anger, Bargaining, Depression,
Acceptance.
It can't be, there's no way, she was supposed to see my wedding
day, she's not dead!
Shut your damn mouth, you have no idea what you're talking
about, you are an absolute idiot.
Come on, there's no way this actually happened is there… Prove it!

It can't be, there's no way, she was supposed to see my wedding
day, she's not dead!
I can't live without her, she was my rock, we used to have lunch
together all the time, all I am, gone, I can't believe it, I won't.
Come on, there's no way this actually happened, is there? Prove it!
She's in a better place, she loved me, I said my goodbyes, I will
always love her.

I can't live without her, she was my rock, we used to have lunch
together all the time, all I am, gone, I can't believe it, I won't.
Shut your damn mouth, you have no idea what you're talking
about, you are an absolute idiot.
Come on, there's no way this actually happened, is there? Prove it!
The Five Stages of Grief; Denial, Anger, Bargaining, Depression,
Acceptance.

Masks

by Catherine Edwins

Put on that mask and start your day.
This is not about you.
This is about the one we've lost.
It is time to honour them.
All the good times we all had…
now naught but a memory.
Do not cry.
Be strong; it's what they would've wanted.
Do not think of them as they were dying.
When you think of them,
Think of them as they were.
Would you want to be remembered
as being weak and withering away
in a pile of your own saliva,
with every last shred of independence torn from you?
No.
Make sure you treat everyone with respect and love
because you never know when it will be
the last time you see them.
When you get to the funeral home,
hold yourself together at all costs.
Everyone there will be sad too.
It's not just you that feels like crying.
Open casket?
Don't be afraid if they don't look like them;
In fact be grateful.
It would be so much harder to say goodbye
if they looked like them.
Closed casket? No problem!
Just keep in mind
that if you're a close family
and organizing the funeral,
you are expected to smile
and nod

and not break down
but you see,
it can be hard to do that sometimes.
Just do your best
and try to do them
as much justice as possible.
When you get home,
after the festivities are long over,
you may remove your mask
and cry yourself to sleep.

by Malea Cruz-Diaz

Set Me Free

by Cory McCulloch

It's not what you gave me, but what you took…
My time… You need to pave the way, you're grim
Your eyes always thin, but you couldn't look
Blind to the sea's beauty, I'd rather swim
You say life ticks like a cracked silver watch
Don't have much in common, get drunk, unwined
My soul is no longer sublime, it's blotched
The heart flew, now it's a caged bird; confined
It isn't too late to repair the pain
Surface of hope, you're my anchor, I sink
Pain, pain, all it does is rattle my brain
Worth all the trouble? Worth the pain? Rethink
We all need to be let go, set me free
Free to dance, free to sing, just let it be

by Zachary Tessaro

Puppet

by Roberta Carriere

I've been whipped into perfection by you
As if I'm a puppet hanging from strings
After time, I know your love was not true
All the pain that's left in my heart still stings
I became your personal Barbie doll
After you left, I had no emotion
You broke me, and then left without a call
With you here, I was under a love potion
I broke free from this curse I was under
I can see the world and be confident
Now I only see the sun, no thunder
My changes of mood is so evident
Now I can live my life with no regret
Relationships no longer seem a threat

by Alysa Cortes

Hope

by Autumn Barnes

Love
forever changing
soul breaking

Miracle
hands intertwining
my mind unwinding

Hope
You had me glowing
Our love was overflowing

Loss
Away from me you went
So did the time we spent

"Reuben" by Tiffany Clarke

Beautiful

by Autumn Barnes

Your curves are beautiful
From your soles
to your messy hair
you are beautiful
Society tries to form
their opinions of you
and what they believe
is beautiful
Change you
Break you
But they don't know
That you already are
Beautiful

by Monika Kobylinska

Melting

by Autumn Barnes

My heart melts like ice cream on a blistering day
Soft whispers lovingly twirl around me
Your warm embrace soothes my trembling nerves
Falling deeper in love every minute we spend

Soft whispers lovingly twirl around me
You are my night and my day
Falling deeper in love every minute we spend
Cherish every moment

You are my night and my day
Your warm embrace soothes my trembling nerves
Falling deeper in love every minute we spend
My heart melts like ice cream on a blistering day

* * *

Unite

by James Dixon

law is injustice
in dangerous times we live
we resist, fight, rise

unseat the corrupt
destroy their platform of hate
remain vigilant

Atomic

by Autumn Barnes

My heart knocked on my chest when you held me
Butterflies infested my sick stomach
I wish you could see what I want to be
Our relationship was so atomic
When you left, a core piece of me left too
Thinking of you daily, hoping you'll call
Mind torture is a lot to put me through
You change so much when drinking alcohol
That night I wish you'd avoided drinking
For five whole years you lay there, unaware
My existence felt like it was sinking
My love, this situation is unfair
After being with you my lesson learned

"Weathered but not Broken" by Mark Gafanha

The Cockroach

by Pepper Dunn-Dufault

A cockroach perches on my back
His insect legs cage my spine
An exoskeleton protecting delicate organs

The cockroach can live for a week without his head
He breathes through microscopic
Holes in his body
Holes in my certainty

Eventually he will die of thirst
Without his foul mouth
And foul words

The cockroach is a poikilotherm
He is cold blooded
His body feels heavy and rigid
And ices over my skin

Cockroach means
Insect that shuns the light
He crawls inside shadows
Waiting to feed

The cockroach clings to my battered frame
Peers over my shoulder
With sick fascination
And erect antennae

I want to throw him off me
Flatten him with earth shattering stomps
Shake the feeling of his weight holding me down
But my body shakes instead
I carry the cockroach

Into change rooms
Where his compound eyes stare back at me from every
mirror

Through dark streets
Where his grotesque wings wrap terror around me

Under my covers
Where he crawls onto my chest and keeps me in bed for
days
Unable to face the world

It has been months since the cockroach infested me
And retreated back into the darkness
From which he came

Yet he will remain
Perched on my back
Forever

Sad Dad

by Cory McCulloch

As I sore in the night sky, you still defy me. Define me.
I try to push you away, but you molded me like the potter's clay.
You don't need to stay... stray.
I know you can't take all the blame, but understand,
you and I are the same.
It's about time for a break, we can't keep up with the heartache.

"Life" by Kenton Tran

Rebirth

by James Dixon

I strengthened my bones from the ghost of myself
My soul was torn from the embers of a flame
Burning away rotten memories
Revealing a layer of raw, fresh skin

My soul was torn from the embers of a flame
Fire washed away my worries
Revealing a layer of raw, fresh skin
I was renewed

Fire washed away my worries
Burning away rotten memories
Revealing a layer of raw, fresh skin
I strengthened my bones from the ghost of myself

"Pensive" by Malea Cruz-Diaz

The Pills

by Roberta Carriere

The pills in my hand
Caused by the demons in my head,
The insecurities I see
When I look in the mirror
Remind me of
The memories of you
When you broke me
Burn in my mind like a fire

As I bring the pills closer
Tears start pouring out of my eyes
like the insults poured out of your mouth.
As if you were a faucet of negativity

I try to be happy but all I am is angry
At me
It could be so much different
If I were different
But I'm me
And it hurts

The pills in my hand
Are now in my mouth.

The Boy

by Johnson Hoang

I had just finished my shift of lifting supplies. My muscles were sore, my slender arm felt like a lead block that I had to drag around. My body had failed to accomplish the simple tasks commanded by my brain such as waving goodbye, walking in a straight line and tilting my head. Everything seemed to be going wrong today, even the air felt suffocating. It had been a long, never ending day. The only thing that I longed for was an end to this pitiful day, however, that didn't happen because on my way home, my brain was lured to the familiar carnival advertisement attached to a light pole. Oddly enough, my fatigued body desired to be at this carnival as it limped all the way to my car.

As I yanked on my car door, the pain slowly subsided. The drive to the carnival lacked any sight of people, animals, or vehicles. The only things visible were the stripes on the road that separated the lanes. When I arrived, the carnival was devoid of colour. I don't know why I came back here. This is where she left me.

There were annoying couples roaming the carnival grounds, lost in their own fantasies. Families weren't capable of controlling their high pitched brats, who were scattered around as if a tarantula egg had hatched. There was a man selling overpriced popcorn. He had neglected to shave his facial monstrosity and left his *Rapunzel*-like hair fall to his lower back. He wore a grease stained shirt, and shorts that revealed his hairy legs. An occasional shriek came from a sorry excuse of a haunted house.

It wasn't until a dart flew through my line of sight that my mind changed its focus to a child, a small tiny shrimp. The child was bright, young, vibrant. He wore a simple blue shirt, red overalls, a yellow fisherman's hat and little yellow rain boots. His gleaming eyes gave me a sense of responsibility. I watched his curiosity grow the more he ran around the carnival. The child exploded into motion as the man with a big red nose created balloon animals. His laughs and giggles were enough to make colours reappear in my vision. He saw brown kernels bloom into golden flowers that aroused his scent. I could tell that he desperately wanted to ride the vehicles that crashed into each other, but he was always caught sneaking into the line by the host who told him, "Someday when you're tall enough buddy." He saw giant plushies that towered over him. He looked at everything with wonder and awe.

Watching the child sprint around the carnival, seeing his amazement at everything he set his eyes upon, was enough for me to feel as if I was on my own adventure.

The station that intrigued him the most was the carousel. The horses, the carriages, the simplicity in their movements was enough for the child to believe that they were racing against time. As the child ran towards the line, he was absorbed into the abyss of strangers. Each time the line moved, the child's thirst for the ride intensified as a rocket lifting off. When the child boarded the carousel, he could not stay still. Adrenaline pumped through his veins as if he were on a sugar rush. Excitement detonated from the child.

The ride commenced. As the carousel picked up speed, the child began to roar, the ride began to roar, the crowd began to roar. I found myself roaring with the entity. This moment made me realize how much time had passed. Everyone on the ride had smiles taking up half of their faces and arms in a victory gesture. Nothing mattered more to me than to see that joy-filled child. One arm gripped the rope of a horse while the other reached out

71

into the crowd surrounding the carousel. The way he extended his arm into the air reminded me that I too, can still find joy in life. The melody of the laughter and screaming danced with the rhythm of the ride, but like all great things, it had to come to an end.

The scene provoked memories that brought me back to a time that made me love life. Where I was once a one of those couples. When I had dreams of having my own family.

The enthusiastic child continued to bounce around the carnival, then suddenly, his joyful world crashed. He turned white as he came to the realization that something was missing. The child desperately looked for help. Our eyes met and the glimmer of hope shone in his eyes, the child approached me asking, "Do you know where my mommy is?"

I replied with in bold voice, hiding any excitement I had. "No, but I'd be happy to help you find her." Together we roamed the carnival like detectives searching for traces of her. Having a partner in crime shorter than my knee fuelled my determination to find the child's parent.

Suddenly the child pulled on my leg and pointed his finger. My eyes were caught once I looked in that direction. My heart stopped. My face turned from pale white to volcanic red. It was her. She wore ripped jeans and a white shirt, overlapped by a burgundy jacket which was all saturated by her scent. The unforgettable scent of her perfume captivated my nose once again. Misery, misery was the only thought that came to mind. She was the vile monster who had abandoned me here.

Why would she come back here? I came to the conclusion that it was for the child's amusement.

The child cried, "Mommy!" as he rushed towards the executioner of love. The monster replied, "Sweetie!" as she bear-hugged the child, attacked him with a barrage of kisses, then proceeded to lift him into the air as if he were *Simba*. Those words and actions, committed by that monster, only stimulated more memories. Memories of watching movies with her, answering her 1:00 a.m. calls, and listening to anything that troubled her. These recollections intensified the atmosphere. The monster was now aware of my presence.

The soft admirable eyes that had looked upon her son, turned into sharp knives that pierced through me. She put her knives back into their sheath and walked away. The child desperately flailed against her to give me his regards, but the grip and daunting glare of the monster had seized him, taking up any happiness that remained within him. The further the child was, the more the colours faded away.

Before I realized it, I was in a colourless world once again. The gloomy air had returned. I felt no sensation from my hand as it stroked my face. I felt no sensation from my heart because the memories of the child failed to fill it up with happiness. I realized that I have nothing more to live for in this dreadful world.

Resentment

by Cory McCulloch

I walk a life in my shoes full of stones
You shed your skin daily like the snake you are
I don't pry like a crowbar
You are a complex puzzle no one wishes to complete
I am my own person
You are a caricature
I don't understand why you seek my approval
You are a pitiful being
I can't wait 'til you fall
You are always crawling back through the dirt
I hate you, and…
You need me

"Rose" by Lucas Bernhard

My Boy

by James Dixon

A father says to his son
Boy,
let me teach you something about life
If you want something, you fight for it

Strong words I heard not directed at me
but I took them as my own
People born the way I was are not taught to fight
They are taught to sit nice, sit still
And silently hope someone wants to fight for you
What other men don't realize is a body
Is not an object to be coveted and won
It's just a vessel for a prophet
a vehicle for an angel

My brain realized at a young age
The body it thought it had and the body it was piloting
Were two different forms, existing
One within and one without
And the reason I hated being seen
Was because other people couldn't see the inner me
My body wasn't a reflection of who I was supposed to be
That is when I knew I wanted something
And I was going to fight for it

A body is a vessel, not an object
But my body was a war that needed to be won
My creator made an error
So I forged my own bones
I turned the stone walls of my prison
Into a bridge to the place sunflowers grow
I created my own liberation
I was born almost two decades ago
But I didn't live until now

My father says to me
My boy,
you taught me something about life

Autumn Songyuio

by Athena Langhorn

Broad oaks and maples host branches as homes
As the sun shines on them so brightly still
For the leaves of the season freely roam
While wild winter winds grow the slightest chill
Leaves dance and flutter in the crisp cool breeze
And as they blow, they journey across the world
Thousands of vividly colourful leaves
In the golden sun, they flutter and twirl
But, there is more to this alluring scene
Lively leaves are battered by blustering air
Sights afterwards are no longer serene
Trees that once hosted the leaves are now bare
Where once there were feathers, orange and red
Now lie remnants, achromatic and dead

by Mimi Hannant-Steffler

Burning Hearts

by Ben Yoganathan

When I was 16, a girl stole my heart for the first time. When I say she stole it, I mean she left the way her hair felt between my fingers in the places I didn't know existed. And when I wasn't looking, she took the part of me that made my stomach turn and my face warm. I used to get sick every time I talked to her.

Our eyes would never meet because I couldn't look at her. But when I did, I felt like the sky was bending towards my face. I told her none of the things I thought in my weird obsessive head. But she snuck her way into every song I listened to, every word I wrote, every night spent not sleeping. Frantic texts and desire jumping off my tongue turned into her, sitting on my couch with me sitting next to her, imagining the least painful way to tell someone you didn't deserve them.

She smelled like home. Words became stuck in my throat and fell to my fingertips as I grabbed her face and pressed it to mine. Everything I didn't say filled the space that no longer existed between our lips. I told her she was beautiful. But only because telling her that she made me want to throw up, and think about death in the best way, might have scared her off. As my chest held her head she filled the silence with the same sheltered words I had carried for so long.

See we are all just living imagining that our friends will one day tear down the home we built together. And no matter how many times someone tells you they love you, we will choose to believe that only emptiness can hold us because it is less painful than to realize the burden of the meaning you provide. Happiness is double-edged; warmth that cuts you where you can't feel any less. Nobody tells you that the moment you find someone who makes your shoulder blades turn into wings, you will also find a way to tear the feathers out of your back. Because the ground is too far. Because they make you look like the person you were always afraid you wanted to be. Because the distance makes you feel sick. Pain is like a warm blanket that you never realize is filling your lungs with the nothing you think you deserve.

Life-and-death are the closest things that exist. You can stop being the emptiness you want to occupy, the moment you look down and realize how shimmering your terror is. Her lips hold me up above anything I ever wanted to soar beyond. If we all opened up our lips with the tears our mothers dropped for us, we could see that we all want nothing, because to love someone is to look away when they take the thing that keeps us bound to our longing. To let them lift us up with the way their hair feels even though there is always a part of us that wants to jump.

Life and death are two edges of the same story. Having something will always make your heart tremble with the emptiness that could be. But isn't that just what it means to be alive? A heart burning.